Charlie Rabbi a Bath

Charlie Rabbit Takes a Bath by Bard Bott

Copyright © 2021. All rights reserved.

ALL RIGHTS RESERVED: No part of this book may be reproduced, stored, or transmitted, in any form, without the express and prior permission in writing of Pen It! Publications, LLC. This book may not be circulated in any form of binding or cover other than that in which it is currently published.

This book is licensed for your personal enjoyment only. All rights are reserved. Pen It! Publications does not grant you rights to resell or distribute this book without prior written consent of both Pen It! Publications and the copyright owner of this book. This book must not be copied, transferred, sold or distributed in any way.

Disclaimer: Neither Pen It! Publications, or our authors will be responsible for repercussions to anyone who utilizes the subject of this book for illegal, immoral or unethical use.

This is a work of fiction. The views expressed herein do not necessarily reflect that of the publisher.

This book or part thereof may not be reproduced in any form, stored in a retrieval system, or transmitted in any form by any means-electronic, mechanical, photocopy, recording or otherwise-without prior written consent of the publisher, except as provided by United States of America copyright law.

Published by Pen It! Publications, LLC in the U.S.A.

812-371-4128   www.penitpublications.com

ISBN: 978-1-63984-048-9

Illustrated by Savannah Horton

Charlie Rabbit likes to be clean.

If he doesn't wash himself throughout the day, his fluffy white fur gets rough and dingy.

He also knows that not washing properly can help multiply the germs.

More germs means it's more likely that Charlie Rabbit will get sick. And Charlie Rabbit doesn't like being sick. So, he always makes sure to take a bath.

Charlie Rabbit can teach us a lot about staying clean.

Even though he doesn't take a bath like we do. He uses his tongue and little paws.

Please don't use your tongue. Your own little paws will do just fine.

Charlie Rabbit knows he needs to wash up before and after eating, after he uses the restroom, and especially after he gets done playing really hard.

When Charlie Rabbit takes a bath, he tries to focus on one area at a time. He will clean each part for at least twenty seconds. Sometimes longer if he is extra dirty.

First, he will wash his front paws, getting between all of his little toes. You can wash your little paws too. Make sure to get between your fingers.

Then, he will wash his face, making sure to get behind his ears. He doesn't want any potatoes to start to grow.

Charlie Rabbit continues washing from his head down to his toes. Stopping in each area to get it extra shiny and clean.

He even makes sure to get his bum and the places in between.

He finishes way down at his lucky rabbit feet. Again, please do not use your tongue, a washcloth will do just fine for you.

If you can't remember when to wash, and scrub, or bathe.

Just think of Charlie Rabbit's plan to wash, and wash, and rinse, and shine.

Then repeat the steps a few times every day.

The Real Charlie

Brad Bott has been writing in one form or another for as long as he can remember. He earned his bachelor's degree in Secondary English Education, which really got him hooked on being a writer. He lives in "the small town," Indiana with his wife Steph and their rabbit, Charlie.

    He is currently a manufacturing shift supervisor. In his off time, he enjoys writing new stories, meeting new people, and traveling.

    Titles from Brad include, *Just One Wish* and *Leprechaun's Luck* (both picture books) and *Salt & Earth* (a poetry collection).

    For more info, visit him on Facebook at Brad Bott Books or visit his blog at <u>bradabott.wordpress.com</u>.

CPSIA information can be obtained
at www.ICGtesting.com
Printed in the USA
BVHW021710160821
614548BV00002B/14